D1103895

FOR WOOD

I just wanted to tell you something about this book. Mrs. Trifle is asleep on the couch in front of the fire and Dr. Trifle has just gone out the back FOR WOOD, so I'll have to make it quick.

I've just read SELBY and I think it's pretty good. (How could it miss, it's about me.) The thing I think you should know is that it's a book of short stories. But they're the kind of stories that are best if you read the first one first and the second one second, and so on. Anyway, here comes Dr. Trifle with a huge log. I'd better stop scribbling before he catches me.

 Selby

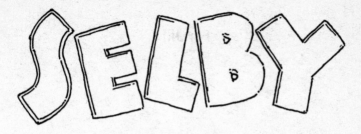

SELBY

The secret adventures of a talking dog

by DUNCAN BALL
illustrated by M. K. Brown

HarperTrophy®
A Division of HarperCollinsPublishers

For Jill

Selby
The Secret Adventures of a Talking Dog
Text adapted from *Selby's Secret*, text copyright 1985,
Selby Screams, text copyright 1989, *Selby Speaks*, text copyright 1988,
and *Selby Supersnoop*, text copyright 1995 by Duncan Ball.
Illustrations copyright © 1997 by M. K. Brown

Printed in the United States of America. For information address
HarperCollins Children's Books, a division of HarperCollins Publishers,
10 East 53rd Street, New York, NY 10022.

Library of Congress Cataloging-in-Publication Data
Ball, Duncan, 1941–
    Selby : the secret adventures of a talking dog / Duncan Ball ;
illustrated by M. K. Brown.
        p.   cm.
    Summary: Follows the adventures of the world's only talking dog as he
tries to keep his talents a secret from his owners.
    ISBN 0-06-440673-3 (pbk.)
    [1. Dogs—Fiction.   2. Humorous stories.]   I. Brown, M. K. (Mary
K.), ill.   II. Title.
PZ7.B1985Se   1997   96-20730
[Fic]—dc20   CIP
                                                                                AC

Typography by Steve Scott
1   2   3   4   5   6   7   8   9   10
❖
First Harper Trophy edition, 1997
Harper Trophy® is a registered trademark
of HarperCollins Publishers Inc.

Contents

Selby's Secret

Selby's secret was that he was the only talking dog in Australia and, perhaps in the world. It wasn't a gift that he was born with. (When he was young he was a perfectly ordinary barking dog.) And it wasn't something that someone taught him. One day he suddenly realized something fantastic had happened to him. Something that would change his life forever.

It all happened one evening when Selby and his owners, the Trifles, were watching a TV program called *Hearthwarm Heath*. It was the story of a butler who worked in a huge mansion. Selby loved the old man because he was so polite and because he knew more about everything than the lord and lady of the house. That night's episode was about an orphan girl who Basil the butler found dying in the snow. He took her into Hearthwarm Hall and looked after her but she kept stealing things and Basil had to pretend that he'd sent her away to the poorhouse—when he really had her hidden in the closet.

Selby had watched television for years. There was never any trouble understanding what was happening. He could always figure it out just from watching. But suddenly, as he blinked back a tear for Basil and the orphan girl, he realized that he understood every word that was being said. He wasn't just looking at the pictures—he knew all the words.

Selby was so shocked that he jumped up and raced around the room saying, "Bow wow wow woof woof yip yipe yip!"—which in dog-talk meant, "I understand every word that is being said! I'm the smartest dog in the world!"—and quickly forgot about the television program.

"For heaven's sake, Selby," Mrs. Trifle said. "It isn't time to eat yet. If you make so much noise, how can we hear the end of *Hearthwarm Heath*?"

"Yipe yipe bow yip yip arrrrr grrrrrr!" Selby said, meaning, "Eat schmeat, I'll show you! I'll show everyone that I understand people-talk! All I have to do is learn to speak it. You'll see!"

From that moment on Selby did everything he could to learn to talk. Whenever the Trifles were out he would sit in front of the TV set repeating everything that was said. His problem was that his mouth just didn't work like a people-mouth. After a lifetime of eating dog food from a bowl and chewing Dry-Mouth Dog Biscuits, Selby's lips simply wouldn't do the things that people-lips did when they spoke. When he tried to say, "Oh bother, Basil, pass me the pepper," it came out, "Oh, gother Gasil, gas gee the gecker."

"I'm going to speak this language," Selby thought, pressing his lips against the spinning clothes dryer to give himself a lip massage after practicing to speak for hours, "even if it kills me. Youch! That's hot!" he yelled, plunging his burning lips into a bucket of water. "I don't know who thought up this dreadful language but you can be sure he didn't eat Dry-Mouth Dog Biscuits. It was probably someone who could drink through a straw and do a proper pucker. In fact if I could just *say* proper pucker I'd be home free."

"Proper pucker, proper pucker, proper pucker," Selby said, but it came out "hocker hucker" every time.

Gradually Selby taught himself to use his lips when he spoke and his dog-accent disappeared. When the Trifles were out of the house he spent hours in front of the hall mirror rattling off the most difficult lip-twisters he knew until, finally, he could say, "Peter Piper picked a peck of pickled peppers" so smoothly that it sounded like the rattle of a distant machine gun.

"Oh, you perfect pooch," Selby said, and then he did a proper pucker and kissed himself in the mirror. "You're my kind of dog."

Selby's plan was simple. He would give the Trifles a Christmas present that they'd never forget. What better present could he give than to tell them his secret? His heart was bursting with joy as he pictured the wonderful scene that would follow as they stood around the fireplace, drinking eggnog, leaning against the wall on one elbow and talking about old times and the wonderful times to come.

And what better way to spring the surprise on them than to wait till they walked in the front door on their way back from the Bogusville Christmas Charity Dinner on Christmas Eve? There, standing just inside the front door and dressed in a suit would be the new Selby; not the old throw-him-a-stick-and-see-if-he-goes-for-it Selby the pet, but the all-new talking friend-of-the-family Selby.

At last it was Christmas Eve and the Trifles were about to return from their dinner. Selby sneaked into Dr. Trifle's wardrobe and got out a white shirt, a tie, and one of the doctor's finest suits. With great

difficulty he slipped the shirt over his head and wrapped the tie once around the collar. Then he put on the top part of the suit.

"I'll skip the slacks," Selby said, seeing that the jacket covered him from neck to tail and putting the pants back in the wardrobe. "They're a bit lacking in the number-of-legs department and, besides, the coat already covers me like a tent."

Selby stood at Mrs. Trifle's dressing-table and did his hair with her hairbrush.

"If a thing's worth doing, it's worth doing right," Selby said, quoting Basil. "I could just look up from my dog-dish one day and say, 'G'day. How's it goin'?' but it really wouldn't be the same, would it?"

Just then Selby heard the Trifles' car pull into the driveway and he dashed to the living room and pulled up a chair just inside the front door. He climbed up, standing on his back legs, and straightened his tie and collar.

"Don't panic, Selby," he told himself, "just remember what you're going to say and say it with feeling: 'Good evening, Madam and Sir,'" he said in his best Basil-the-butler voice, "'and a very merry Christmas to you both.'"

Selby's heart raced with excitement as the Trifles crunched their way along the gravel path.

"It's on nights like this," he heard Mrs. Trifle

6

say, "that I wish we had a butler to give us an after-dinner snack and a pot of tea."

"Oh, it's so exciting! If this takes much longer I think I'll explode!" Selby squealed, looking in the mirror and deciding that—but for the long ears and hairy face—he looked quite a lot like Basil himself. "Hurry up! I can't wait any longer!"

"It's a pity," Dr. Trifle said, putting his key in the lock and opening the door a crack, "that we couldn't give Selby a few things to do around the house. If he could only understand us he'd be very useful. We might even send him on errands."

"You do have a wild imagination," Mrs. Trifle laughed. "A talking dog. Fancy Selby actually talking."

"Hmmmmmm," Selby hmmmmmmed and his mind raced like a windmill.

"If we could teach the poor old thing to talk," Dr. Trifle said, "we could get him to answer the telephone and take messages when we're out."

"Hmmmmmmm . . . ," Selby hmmmmmmed again and suddenly his heart skipped a beat. "Poor old thing indeed," he thought. "They don't want a pet, they want a servant—and I'm about to be it! They'll have me running around like Basil the butler! Help!"

Selby thought of tearing back to the bedroom

7

and hiding the clothes but it was too late. The door swung open and Dr. and Mrs. Trifle stared at him with their mouths open.

"Selby!" Mrs. Trifle screamed. "What's got into you?! What do you think you're doing?!"

Selby stood for an instant, frozen like a statue, and then he jumped down and raced around the room with Dr. Trifle's clothes flying everywhere. And as he ran he gave the only answer he could possibly give: "Arf! Arf! Arf! Arf! Aroooooooo!" All of which in dog-talk means, "Good evening, Madam and Sir, and a very merry Christmas to you both."

And so Selby's secret remained a secret—at least for the moment.

Lucky Millions

"Poor Mrs. Trifle," Selby thought as he lay alone in the house (curled up in the beanbag chair) watching *The Lucky Millions Quiz Show*. "It really isn't fair. She works so hard. If only I could earn a lot of money and give it to her. Then she could have a real vacation."

No sooner were these words out of his mouth than Larry Limelight, the host of *The Lucky Millions Quiz Show*, said something that made Selby leap to his feet: "And now," Larry screamed, flashing a set of teeth that looked like the keys of a grand piano, "we have a super-duper special for all you folks at home. This new feature is called the Special Viewers' Phone-in Holiday History Question. The first person to phone in the correct answer to this question will win a vacation for two on a yacht on the Barrier Reef. Listen carefully now," Larry said, lowering his voice nearly to a

9

whisper. "The question is: what country did Napoleon crown himself king of in 1804?"

"I know it! I know it!" Selby yelled as he ran to the phone and dialed *Lucky Millions,* thinking all the while about the TV program he had seen three weeks before called *Napoleon: The Long and the Short of Him.*

Selby listened as the phone rang and he watched Larry Limelight on TV picking up the receiver.

"The answer," Selby said coolly before Larry Limelight could open his mouth, "is . . . nothing."

Selby watched the host's smile fade.

"I'm terribly sorry," the man said, "your answer is incorrect. But thank you for being a good sport. We'd like to send you a special *Lucky Millions* T-shirt—"

"Hold your T-shirt, Larry," Selby said. "Napoleon didn't become king of anything in 1804. He became *emperor* of France in 1804 and king of Italy in 1805."

Larry Limelight read the card in his hand and flashed a blinding smile.

"Yes!" he screamed. "You've got it! You've just won a glorious trip for two to the fabulous Barrier Reef on the yacht of your dreams. Now could I please have your name?"

"Name *(gulp)* . . . ah, er . . . let's see now," Selby said.

"We have to have your name to send you the tickets," Larry Limelight said with a laugh.

"Well . . . of course," Selby said. "I'm Dr. Trifle of number five Bunya-Bunya Crescent, Bogusville."

"Way out there in Bogusville!" Larry said. "That's great!"

"Yes, and while you're at it, could you please include my dog Selby on these tickets. Mrs. Trifle and I never travel without our dog," Selby said, adding, "he's a wonderful dog and we just wouldn't know what to do—"

"No problem," Larry Limelight said, putting the phone down. "The man never travels without his dog. Isn't that great! Now let's get on with the show!"

"I did it!" Selby screamed as he danced around the room. "I really did it!" and then he started singing the *Lucky Millions* theme song:

Love that money madness,
See those dollars drifting down,
Sing away your troubles,
Hang upside down.

The next day Selby looked out the front window in time to see a man with the *Lucky Millions* crest

11

on his blazer tramp through a bed of petunias on the way to the house.

"Uh-oh, what's this?" Selby said, feeling lucky that Mrs. Trifle was out at a council meeting and Dr. Trifle was at the Bogusville Memorial Rose Garden working on the floral clock. "Why is he coming here? I thought they were going to *send* the tickets."

"Dr. Trifle!" the man called out, pounding his fist on the front door. "Open up! I have your vacation tickets."

"Slide them under the door," Selby called back.

"You can't have the tickets till you sign the form."

"What form?" Selby asked. "Nobody said anything about a form."

"It's the one that says that *Lucky Millions* isn't responsible if the yacht sinks and you drown. Just a formality, of course. Now open up please, I've got to get back to the city."

"I can't open the door," Selby said, searching the corners of his brain for reasons why he couldn't open the door.

"Why not?"

"The house is quarantined," Selby said, putting on a raspy voice. "I have *(mumble mumble)* fever and no one's allowed to come near me."

"What kind of fever?" the man asked.

"I have," Selby shouted and then he let his voice drop again and he put a paw over his mouth, "(*mumble mumble*) fever."

"I still can't hear you. It sounds like *mumble mumble* fever."

"It's doodlyboop fever," Selby said, "and it's very catching."

"I've never heard of doodlyboop fever."

"Most people who hear of it are dead by dinner-time," Selby said. "Just push the paper under the door and I'll sign it."

"I can't get it under," the man said, crumpling the paper as he tried. "There's not enough room."

"Okay. I'll open the door and go into my study. Just give the paper to my dog and he'll bring it to me," Selby said. "But I warn you, don't set foot in the house if you know what's good for you."

Selby unlocked the door and let the breeze blow it slowly open.

"Here you go, mutt," the man said, thrusting the paper into Selby's mouth and giving him a slap on the behind as he turned to go. "Get that stupid man to sign the thing. I've got to get cracking. It's a long way back to civilization."

Selby dashed into the darkened study, hopped on the chair, and turned on the desk lamp to read the small print on the form.

"Mutt, schmutt," Selby said, angry at the slap

on the behind and at the man calling Dr. Trifle stupid. "Well the form seems all right. I'll just sign it and get rid of him."

Selby signed the paper using his best imitation of the doctor's handwriting. He had folded it and put it in his mouth when suddenly the shadow of the *Lucky Millions* man fell across the desk.

"Hey!" the man said. "What's going on here! Where's Dr. Trifle?"

Selby turned his head slowly and looked at the man.

"In a second," he thought, "he'll know that Dr. Trifle isn't here. In another second he'll know the horrible truth: that I'm the only reading, writing, and talking dog in all of Australia and, perhaps in the world. This could be my last second of freedom. I've got to act fast."

The man snatched the paper from Selby's mouth just as Selby's paw hit the button on the desk lamp and threw the room into darkness. Before the man's eyes could adjust to the dark, Selby yelled, "Get out of here, you fool! Get out before my dog rips you to pieces!"

Selby growled and sank his teeth into the man's leg as he ran out of the study and straight out the front door and through the petunias.

"Help! Call off your dog!" the man cried as he

leaped into his car, throwing the envelope with the tickets in it out the window as he sped away.

"Silly man," Selby said, spitting out a piece of the man's pants and picking up the envelope. "Why do people have to make life so difficult?"

Finished in a Flash

"What a great camera!" Dr. Trifle said as he whipped around and snapped a picture of the bewildered Selby. "It's amazing! All you have to do is point it and press the button and it does everything else. It focuses itself and decides if it needs the flash and it even winds the film!"

"That was a close call," Selby thought, as he looked up from the newspaper he'd been lying on. "He almost caught me secretly reading. I've got to be very careful with Dr. Trifle snapping pictures with his new Inig-Matic camera or my secret won't be a secret for much longer."

"Look at all these exciting features!" Dr. Trifle said, reading the camera brochure about all the buttons that could be pressed and dials that could be turned. "It's even got Smile-Sensitivity!"

"Smile-Sensitivity?" Mrs. Trifle asked as she wondered why men were so interested in pressing buttons and turning dials. "Does that mean you'll hurt its feelings if you smile at it?"

"Nothing of the kind," Dr. Trifle said. "It's something special that lets you press a button on the back of the camera and then run around to the front and it takes your picture—but not until you smile. Isn't that great!"

"And what if you don't feel like smiling?" asked Mrs. Trifle.

"Then it'll refuse to take your picture."

"Refuse to take your picture?" Mrs. Trifle said. "How dare it? I may be a bit old-fashioned but, the way I see it, cameras should do what you tell them to do."

"That's all well and good for your normal run-of-the-mill camera. But these new cameras have minds of their own. If it's set for Smile-Sensitivity you'd better smile or it'll just jam up and that's that, no picture."

"Perhaps I'm missing the point," Mrs. Trifle said.

"The point is that cameras don't lie."

"Is that so?" Mrs. Trifle thought as she tried to remember if she'd ever been lied to by a camera.

"That just means that if someone is feeling sad or looking terrible or something, it'll come out in the photo. But if you click the Smile-Sensitivity button, this one will only take happy photos," Dr. Trifle said as he clipped his Super Bug-O-Rama magnifying lens on the front of the camera. "Now I'm going out to the garden to get some pictures of insects."

"But we've got to go shopping now," Mrs. Trifle said. "Besides, how will you ever get a bug to smile?"

"That's silly," Dr. Trifle laughed, and with this he spun around and took another snapshot of Selby, almost catching him reading again. "You don't turn on the Smile-Sensitivity when you're taking pictures of insects."

"This thing's driving me crazy," Selby thought, picking up the camera when Dr. and Mrs. Trifle had gone shopping. "I can't do anything for fear of being photographed. Even if I'm lying innocently in front of the TV Dr. Trifle might take a picture. When it was developed he might realize that I was actually watching the TV."

Selby pushed some buttons and turned some dials on the camera and then picked up the brochure. It showed a picture of a camera sliced down the middle and lots of arrows pointing to things.

"This camera *does* have everything," Selby thought, getting more interested by the minute. "It's even got a shark alarm for when you're taking pictures underwater."

The thought of swimming underwater with the Inig-Matic dangling from his neck suddenly brought a smile to Selby's lips and—just as suddenly—there was a blinding flash.

"What was that?" Selby said, dropping the brochure and hoping the flash was lightning striking or a lightbulb burning out. "Oh, no! I forgot about the Smile-Sensitivity. It's taken a picture of me reading the brochure! When the Trifles see the photograph, they'll know I can read! My secret will be out! Help! I've got to do something fast!"

Selby lunged for the camera to destr
but just then Dr. Trifle burst in the door

"Goodness," the doctor said as he gr
camera from in front of the flying dog.
is finished. I'll have to send it away to Celia's to be
processed straight away."

That night Selby couldn't sleep.

"I'm sitting on a time bomb," he thought. "As
soon as Dr. Trifle gets his pictures back in the mail,
he'll see the one of me reading and my days of
freedom will be over. Oh, sure, at first it'll be all
friendly. They'll ask me what it's like to be a dog
and I'll tell them how horrible Dry-Mouth Dog
Biscuits are and they may even give me some of
their own people-food to eat. Then, gradually, there
will be things to be done. 'Selby, would you mind
doing this and would you mind doing that?' Before
I know it, I'll be their servant! I want to be their pet,
not their servant. Or worse still, they'll send me off
to a laboratory where I'll have to talk to boring sci-
entists all day. Oh woe, woe, woe. The only sen-
sible thing is to snitch the photo and the negative
before Dr. Trifle sees them. But how?"

For the next few days when Postman Paterson
put the mail in the Trifles' mailbox, Selby was
watching from the garage through Dr. Trifle's binoc-
ulars.

21

That's it!" Selby said at last when he saw the unmistakable yellow envelope from Celia's No-Scratch Photo Service. "Now if I can only get to the envelope . . ."

Selby crept out to the mailbox and nudged the lid up with his nose as he often did when he brought in the mail. But just as he was about to grab the envelope, a hand shot in front of his face and beat him to it.

"Never mind, Selby," said Dr. Trifle, who'd also been anxiously waiting for the postman's delivery. "I'll get it. Yooohooo!" he called over to Mrs. Trifle. "Come and have a look at the photos!"

The sweat dripped from Selby's forehead as Dr. and Mrs. Trifle looked through the stack of photographs.

"Isn't that a good one of you?" Mrs. Trifle said to Mr. Trifle.

"What do you mean?" Dr. Trifle said. "It makes me look terrible."

"Well they say the camera doesn't lie, dear," Mrs. Trifle chuckled as her husband flipped through the pack.

"My goodness! What's this?" Dr. Trifle suddenly exclaimed as he looked at the last picture.

"I do believe it's Selby!" Mrs. Trifle said, looking over at Selby who was lying innocently on the ground.

"I can't stand it," Selby thought as he cleared his throat. "I'll have to tell them. They've caught me. I'll have to confess. *Gulp*."

"But how could he have taken it?" Mrs. Trifle asked.

"Well I don't know," Dr. Trifle said, frowning at Selby. "Maybe he just bumped against it and *flash!* it went off."

For a minute, Dr. and Mrs. Trifle's heads went back and forth from the photo to Selby like two people watching a tennis match.

"It's really quite extraordinary," Mrs. Trifle said. "I can't imagine how it happened."

"I must have left the Super Bug-O-Rama magnifying lens on the camera," Dr. Trifle said. "It just looks like a close-up of fur with a tiny piece of his collar showing. What a laugh."

"Thank goodness," Selby thought as he breathed a great sigh of relief. "Cameras may not lie but luckily for me they don't always tell the whole truth either."

Selby Supersnoop, Dog Detective

Selby was all alone and bored silly. There was nothing on TV and no good books to read. Or were there?

Selby climbed to the top shelves of the bookcase in the study to see if there were any books he hadn't read. Just when he was about to climb down again, he spied a dusty old book. It was *The Art of the Private Investigator* by Mary Touchstone, P.I.

"Very interesting," Selby thought as he flicked the book off the shelf with his paw and let it crash to the floor. "I've always wanted to be a detective."

In a second, Selby was curled up on the couch reading the back cover. As he read, his jaw began to quiver with excitement.

Thrill to the mystery, romance, and adventure of the world of the private investigator! Amaze

your friends! Have your enemies arrested! Earn
big money in crime detection and have a great
time! Don't waste another minute. Read this
book and your life will be changed forever!

"Mystery, romance, and adventure, wow!"
Selby squealed. "That really makes a medium-sized
dog's spine tingle. I can't wait to have my life
changed forever!"

With trembling paws, Selby opened the book
and began to read:

Anyone can become a private investigator, or
P.I. as we are known. So settle back, follow
this easy step-by-step guide, and soon you will
be solving mysteries all over your neighbor-
hood.

"I'm settled back, Mary," Selby said out loud,
"and ready to solve mysteries all over my neigh-
borhood. I can't wait!"

All afternoon Selby read through chapters called
"How to Be a Master of Disguise," "How to Spot
a Criminal," "How to Tail a Suspect," "How to Find
Clues," "How to Overpower People," and "How
to Eavesdrop." It was all there: everything Selby had
always wanted to know about solving crimes and
catching criminals.

Finally Selby read the last paragraph in the book:

Just remember that the world of the private investigator is the world of mystery. Nothing is the way it seems. Look for clues everywhere and suspect everyone and you can't go wrong. Happy detecting!

"What a great book!" Selby cried. "But where am I going to find my first case? Bogusville is such a boring place. There's never any crime or anything."

But Selby had spoken too soon. The very next day, just when Selby was wondering how he could use his new detective knowledge, there came a knock at the Trifles' door.

"Excuse me, Dr. Trifle," the woman said, "my name is Eve Amery."

"The toy soldier collector," Dr. Trifle said, snapping his fingers. "I saw something about you in the newspaper years ago. Come right in."

"They're *model* soldiers. They're not really toys."

"How may I help you?"

"There's been a crime committed and I need your help."

Selby's head shot out from behind the couch.

"A crime!" he thought. "An actual real live crime here in Bogusville!"

27

"What crime?" Dr. Trifle asked.

"Someone is stealing my model soldiers," Eve said. "Let me explain. Emery—he's my brother—and I live in a house across town. The soldiers were our grandfather's and when our parents died, they became ours."

"They're fighting a battle, I believe."

"Yes, in a big glass case with hills and trees and trenches. Recently Emery and I decided to sell them but suddenly they started disappearing."

"Disappearing?" Dr. Trifle said.

"Disappearing," Selby thought.

"Someone is stealing them," Eve said. "Every Tuesday some more are missing. Every week there are fewer and fewer. There are practically none left."

"Have you been to the police?" Dr. Trifle asked.

"Yes, and they were very helpful. But they don't think anyone is breaking in. We have locks on our doors and bars on all the windows, you see."

"Then what's happening?"

"I'm ashamed to say that the police think that Emery—my own dear brother—is taking the soldiers, Dr. Trifle."

"But why would he steal what he already owns?"

"No, no, *we* own them. The police think he's selling them and keeping all the money for himself.

Every Tuesday evening he catches the bus to the city to visit friends, you see. He could be taking the soldiers then."

"Why don't the police arrest him?"

"Because they have no proof."

"I see," Dr. Trifle said. "So you think that because I'm an inventor I might have an invention that could tell if your brother is taking the soldiers?"

"Do you?" she asked with a smile.

"Possibly. May I see one of these soldiers?"

Eve Amery handed three soldiers to Dr. Trifle who studied them carefully.

"Got it!" he said. "Each soldier has a hole down the middle. We could slip a little specially charged magnetic strip in there where no one will see it. Then we hide my Super-Sensitive Magnetic Screaming Theft Detector in the bushes outside your house. If anyone walks by with a soldier then—"

Dr. Trifle let out a loud, wailing, machine-like scream. Eve Amery and Selby covered their ears till he stopped.

"That's marvelous," Eve said. "May I see this Super-Sensitive Magnetic Screaming Theft Detector of yours, Dr. Trifle?"

"Yes, of course. As soon as I've made one. I just thought it up a minute ago. But don't worry; I'll have one ready by Tuesday."

That night Selby lay awake listening as Dr. Trifle worked on his new invention.

"This is great!" Selby thought. "Now all we have to do is spring the trap and catch Eve's brother in the act! Hey, that almost rhymes!"

On Tuesday evening, Dr. Trifle and Sergeant Short hid in the bushes as Eve Amery said goodbye to her brother. None of them knew that Selby had sneaked across town and was hiding in a tree nearby.

"This is so exciting!" he thought. "I'm a real snoop now!"

Just then, Emery walked down the path and the lights, horns, and bells in Dr. Trifle's Super-Sensitive Magnetic Screaming Theft Detector flashed and honked and tinkled all at once.

"What's that noise?" Emery screamed.

"I'm afraid you're under arrest," Sergeant Short said, stepping out of the bushes.

"For what?"

"For stealing model soldiers and taking them to the city to sell."

"You've got to be kidding," Emery said. "I don't give two hoots for those stupid things. I wouldn't be caught dead with one!"

By now, Dr. Trifle was pointing a second invention, his new Miniature Hand-Held Super-Sensitive Magnetic Pinging Theft Detector, at Emery's left-hand coat pocket and it was going *ping ping ping* so fast that it sounded like the international Ping-Pong play-offs.

"What's in that pocket?" Sergeant Short asked.

"Nothing," Emery said, reaching in and pulling out five soldiers. "Hey! How'd they get in there? This is a set-up! You put them in there!"

"I'm afraid you'll have to come with us," the policeman said.

Selby watched as Dr. Trifle and the policeman led Emery Amery away.

"Poor Eve," Selby thought, sniffing a little sniff. "She *thought* her brother was taking the soldiers but *knowing* is different. She must be grief-stricken."

Selby was about to climb down from the tree when something in *The Art of the Private Investigator* came back to him.

"'Nothing is the way it seems,'" he quoted. "'Suspect everyone and you can't go wrong.'"

"Hey now, hold the show!" Selby thought. "What if Emery isn't guilty? What if someone—his sister, for example—put the soldiers in his pocket?"

From where Selby sat he could just barely see in the window of the house. There was music playing and suddenly Eve Amery danced by, leaping and letting out a series of *whooooopeeeees!*

"If this woman's grief-stricken, then I'm a baboon's bottom!" Selby thought. "Something very strange is going on around here."

The music stopped and Selby saw Eve Amery dash to the telephone.

"I'd love to hear what she's saying," Selby thought, as he remembered the chapter of the book on how to eavesdrop. "If only I could get into the house and listen in. If I can get from this branch to the roof maybe I could pull up a bit of roofing and climb in," Selby thought, remembering the chapter called "How Burglars Burgle."

Quietly as a cat, Selby lowered himself onto the roof, pulled up a bit of roofing, and climbed into the house. Through the ceiling he could hear Eve talking on the telephone in the room below.

". . . no more problems now that my stupid brother is out of the way. I'll be on a plane and out of the country as soon as he's in jail. They're all mine to sell now! All mine! He'll never catch up to me!"

"Mary Touchstone, P.I., was right," Selby thought as he crawled towards a crack in the ceiling to see down. "But how will I tell the police that Eve framed her brother?"

Selby moved forward again and felt something jab his paw.

"Ouch!" he cried in plain English. "That hurt!"

There was dead silence below. Selby squinted in the darkness and saw that he'd stepped on a little model soldier. Around him in the darkness he now saw dozens more.

"So this is where she hid them!" Selby thought.

Suddenly Eve, hearing Selby's cry, stood on a chair and opened the secret trapdoor in the ceiling, all of which would have been okay if Selby hadn't been standing on it at the time. In a second, the door swung down and Selby dropped straight onto the woman, knocking her to the floor unconscious.

"Now I'll just call the police," Selby said, getting up and shaking off a dozen model soldiers.

In a second, he was speaking to Sergeant Short.

"I have some important information about the Amery case," Selby said, putting on a deep detective-like voice. "Emery is innocent."

"Really?"

"Yes, really. His sister, Eve, planted those soldiers on him. She hid the others in the ceiling of their house. She was going to sell them and keep all the money for herself."

"Who are you?" Sergeant Short asked.

"Never mind who I am," Selby said. "Just get over to the Amerys' house right away and you'll find Eve asleep on the floor."

"We're on our way," the policeman said. "But tell us how you found all this out."

"I listened in on a telephone conversation she was having." Selby said. "That's what tipped me off."

"You were listening in? You mean you eavesdropped?"

"You can bet your boots I did," Selby laughed. "You should have seen me—I dropped right on top of Eve!"

Raid on Planet Kapon

"Oh, wow!" Selby said, reading the entertainment page of the *Bogusville Banner* and seeing that the movie *Raid on Planet Kapon* had finally come to the Bogusville Bijou. "I've got to see it! I'll wait till Dr. and Mrs. Trifle are asleep and sneak out to the late show."

Selby waited outside the theater till the movie was about to begin and then crept in in the dark and found a seat in the back row where no one would notice him. In a minute the film started with a roll of drums and some *ping ping ping zip* noises and then a crash of cymbals. Across the screen in a great burst of swirling galaxies and exploding stars came the title of the movie:

**REVOLT OF THE UNIVERSE
EPISODE EIGHT:
RAID ON PLANET KAPON**

"Fantabulous!" Selby said, hanging his paws over the empty seat in front of him. "I've seen all the other movies in the series and this one is supposed to be the best of all of them!"

Then a lot of words came up on the screen, getting bigger as they went, and a deep voice read them out at the same time:

> *Prince Zak and Princess Su have made their way to Planet Kapon to live in peace after the end of the Third Galactic War. They have the all-powerful Star Web which was given to them by the Mighty Master of the Universe before he died. With the Star Web safely in the hands of the prince and princess the Universe will remain good and nice and its people will be able to do as they please forever. But little do they know, Lord Dar Coarse is gathering together the Forces of the Darkened Light to raid Planet Kapon and steal the Star Web.*

"Crikey!" Selby said as another star exploded on the screen. "I thought Lord Dar Coarse was killed when he fell screaming into the sun at the end of the last movie."

"The time has come to crush Prince Zak and Princess Su," Lord Dar Coarse said to his evil robot

36

Yor Wun 2. "I don't want any accidents this time. Do you hear! No accidents! Let's get going."

Lord Dar Coarse and his fleet of hundreds of starships sped through time and space till they reached Planet Kapon. Then, hovering in the darkness above the tiny planet, Lord Dar Coarse pressed a button that said FORCE FIELD and suddenly all the lights in the houses on Planet Kapon went off, including the nightlight in the bubble house where Prince Zak and Princess Su lay sleeping.

Lord Dar Coarse's starship drifted silently down to the surface of the planet while the other ships stayed behind.

"Wake up!" Selby said, almost loud enough to be heard above the music. "They're coming to get the Web!"

Lord Dar Coarse and Yor Wun 2 got out of their ship and stood for a moment in the darkness outside the prince and princess's house. The villains took out their light sabers and were ready to burst in through the door when suddenly the prince and princess appeared on the top of the bubble above them.

"The force of right! The freedom of might!" Prince Zak yelled (as he always did), and he threw the Star Web—which looked to Selby like the net that Phil Philpot put over his peach tree to keep the birds from eating his peaches, only the Star Web glittered with blue light—over Lord Dar Coarse and Yor Wun 2.

"Great stuff!" Selby said, climbing right up onto the back of the seat to get a better view. "This is so exciting! This is wonderful!"

Just when the prince and princess were escaping from the planet with the Star Web, the movie suddenly stopped and the theater went completely black except for the manager's flashlight.

"Ladies and gentlemen," the manager said, "I regret to say that the power has gone off all over Bogusville. You may wait for a while and see if it comes on again and we can finish the movie, or come to the box office and I'll give you your money back. I'm sorry for the inconvenience."

"What a disappointment," Selby thought as he shot past the ticket office without stopping to get back the money which he hadn't paid anyway. "I'd better go home. It could be hours till the power comes back on."

Selby was on his way through the middle of Bogusville when he noticed two dark figures standing in the road. They both held flashlights with long red cones on their ends.

"I don't want any accidents this time," one of the men said in a low voice. "Let's get going."

"Crikey!" Selby said, stopping dead in his tracks. "That's what Lord Dar Coarse said to Yor Wun 2! Oh, no! Look at the light sabers! It's them! They've shut off the power with their force field! I'd better tell the police."

Selby tore back to the police station to find Constable Long and Sergeant Short, but the building was empty.

"They've captured the cops already!" Selby said. "I'll have to take matters into my own paws."

Selby raced to Phil Philpot's house and pulled the net off the peach tree.

"I don't have the Star Web so this will have to do," he said as he ran back to the spot where the two men stood in the road.

Then, holding the net in his mouth, Selby crept up a tree and walked quietly out on a limb that hung over the men.

Suddenly Selby yelled out in plain English: "The forces of right! The freedom of might!"—only it sounded more like: "The gorses of gright! The greedom of gite!" with his mouth full of net—and with this he dropped the net down over the two men and jumped after it.

"I've got you now, Lord Dar Coarse," Selby said, winding the net around the two struggling men. "And as for your evil robot, you can kiss him

39

goodbye. He'll be nothing but nuts and bolts when I'm finished."

"Hey! Who is that?" the men yelled. "What's going on?"

Just then the lights of Bogusville went back on revealing Constable Long and Serveant Short tangled in the net with their traffic torches still glowing. Selby looked at the policemen and backed slowly away thinking of a thousand places he'd rather be at the moment.

"Hey!" yelled Sergeant Short, looking right at Selby. "Isn't that Mayor Trifle's dog?"

"Why yes it is," Constable Long said, pulling the net off them. "He must have been right here when this happened. He probably saw the person who did it."

"Yeah," said Sergeant Short. "If only dogs could talk, I think someone would have some serious explaining to do."

"Gulp," Selby thought as he dashed back to the Bijou to see the rest of *Raid on Planet Kapon.* "If the lights had come on two seconds sooner, *I'd* be the one doing the serious explaining."

Number Fumbler

"Remember when the council chose the town of Twin Castles in Tallstoria to be our sister town?" Mrs. Trifle, who was the mayor of Bogusville, asked Dr. Trifle.

"Yes," Dr. Trifle said. "As I recall, the mayor of Twin Castles was planning to come here for a visit sometime."

"Not just sometime," Mrs. Trifle said. "Count Karnht and his wife, the countess, will be staying here for the night tonight. They're due at five o'clock."

"How exciting! I do hope he speaks English. I don't speak a word of Tallstorian."

"Count Karnht speaks perfect English but he has trouble with his numbers. He has a way of saying two when he means one and three when he means four and so on."

"You mean, Count Karnht can't count?"

"Yes. He grew up very rich and always had other people to count for him so he never learned. But Countess Karnht can count and she's written to tell us to ignore anything that her husband says that has numbers in it."

"My goodness," Dr. Trifle said, as a huge black car with flags on it pulled into the driveway. "I think it's them!"

"The count that can't count can't tell time either," thought Selby as he noticed the royal couple were two hours early.

"Let's not be formal," Count Karnht said, kissing Dr. and Mrs. Trifle on both cheeks. "We're not here as the royal single—"

"He means the royal *couple,*" the countess whispered to the Trifles.

"—but as the mayor of Triple Castles."

"He means *Twin* Castles," the countess said. "And I *do* apologize if we're early or late. My husband said we were due at fifteen o'clock and I took a wild guess that he meant three."

"It's six dozen of one or half of another," the count said, suddenly seeing Selby and screaming: "Help! Get that three-legged creature out of here! I was attacked by two packs of them when I was a boy of thirty."

"But Selby wouldn't hurt a fly," Mrs. Trifle said.

"I don't care how many flies he wouldn't hurt,"

Count Karnht said, jumping up on the table. "I can't cope with dogs. My wife used to keep canines but we had to get rid of them. They frighten me out of my wit!"

"You mean, your *half* wit," Selby thought as he slinked out the door which Dr. Trifle held open for him. "Now *I've* got to sleep outside just because Count Karnht who can't count can't cope with canines."

Selby went down to Bogusville Creek, curled up in a bush and slept for a couple of hours—which would have been okay if Count Karnht hadn't come along on his evening walk and stood throwing stones in the water.

"I can't seem to get away from him," Selby said to himself.

"Another dog!" Count Karnht cried, seeing Selby and jumping into a deep part of the creek.

"What a ninny," Selby thought as he got up slowly and stretched. "I guess I'd better get out of here before this turns into an international incident."

"Heeeeelp!" yelled the count.

"Now wait a minute," Selby thought as he turned to go. "The count's gone under and he hasn't come up! In a minute he could be the drowned Count Karnht!"

Selby watched as the count bobbed to the surface and thrashed around with his arms.

"Learning to count wasn't the only thing the count didn't learn to do when he was young," Selby thought. "It seems he didn't learn much about swimming either."

Selby thought for a minute about diving into the creek and grabbing the count by the collar.

"It'll never work," he thought. "He's too frightened. He'd just pull us both under. Besides, I can't swim, either. I could hold out a branch for him to grab," Selby thought, spying a long branch lying nearby, "but no matter what I do, he'll know I'm not just an ordinary dog! My secret will be out! But I can't let him drown . . ."

Selby grabbed the branch and held it out but the floundering count was too frightened to grab it.

"Don't panic, your moronic majesty!" Selby said suddenly. "Just grab the branch!"

"Good gracious!" sputtered the count. "You talked!"

"Never mind about that," Selby said, leaning further out.

Selby pulled the count to shore just as the whole of the Bogusville police force—Constable Long and Sergeant Short—came running.

"What's wrong?" Constable Long asked. "What's the fuss?"

"It's all right now, officers," the count said, coughing out some water and wiping his eyes. "A nice dog frightened me into the water but then he rescued me so it was okay."

"You were rescued by a dog?" Constable Long said. "What sort of dog?"

"A dog sort of a dog," the count said, looking around for Selby who'd run back into the bushes. "You know, the kind with five legs."

"A five-legged dog?" Sergeant Short asked.

"Yes, of course," the count said, combing his hair back, "and three ears and two heads. You know perfectly well what I mean and don't pretend you don't!"

Constable Long pulled out a pad of paper and a pencil.

"Let's see," he said, making some notes. "You were rescued by a dog with five legs, three ears, and two heads. Just an ordinary dog, was it?"

"Good heavens, no!" the count said sharply. "There was nothing ordinary about him. He talked to me in perfect English."

"He *talked*?" Sergeant Short said.

"He certainly did. Now, if you don't mind, I am His Highnesses Count Karnht, the mayor of Quadruple Castle in Tallstoria," Count Karnht said, pulling out a soggy mayor's ribbon and putting it around his neck. "I'm staying with your mayor, Mrs. Trifle. Now take me to her house on the triple."

The two policemen stared at each other in disbelief.

"Oh, so you're Count Karnht who can't count," Constable Long said.

"That, certainly, is I," the count said, standing up very straight.

"Very well then, Count, we'll take you back to the mayor's house. I know it's in Bunya-Bunya Crescent but I've forgotten the number," Constable Long said, winking at Sergeant Short. "You wouldn't remember what it was, would you?"

"Why yes, I think I do. It was either a thousand hundred or zero two six. Either way I know it had an eight in it," Count Karnht said as he climbed into the police car. "It's a pity that dog left so quickly. I wanted to say, 'Thanks.'"

"I'm sure he'd have wanted to say, 'You're welcome,'" Constable Long said, holding back a giggle.

"I'm sure of it," the count said. "Now let's get going. My pant is wringing wet and so are my shirts."

"Fortunately the count and countess will be leaving tomorrow morning," Selby said, as the police car drove away. "So, in the meantime, I think I'll just stay here and catch thirty winks. *Thirty winks?* Oh, no! Now he's got me doing it!"

47

Selby Supersnout

It all began the day that Selby read the chapter in *The Art of the Private Investigator* on using dogs to sniff out clues.

"I'd be a hopeless sniffer-dog," Selby thought as he sniffed his way around the house. "I couldn't find a rotten fish in a room full of roses. And all this dust makes me feel like a four-legged vacuum cleaner. *Achoooo!*"

That afternoon Dr. and Mrs. Trifle received an invitation to the launch of a fabulously expensive new perfume made by the famous perfume-maker, Pierre de Paris of the House of Pierre Perfumerie.

"I know they launch ships," said Dr. Trifle, "but I didn't know they launched perfumes.'

"It's really just a big party to tell everyone about the perfume," Mrs. Trifle explained.

"They've hired the movie theater for the evening. This new perfume is called Composure."

"Composure? What an odd name," Dr. Trifle said. "Why don't they call it Morning Rose or Evening Daffodil—something that smells like something?"

"These days perfumes have much more interesting names like Quest, and React, and Lightning, and Composure. The names have nothing to do with the smell anymore."

"If you ask me, I think it's all very silly," Dr. Trifle said. "People should spend their money on more useful things."

"It's really just a bit of fun," Mrs. Trifle said. "And I'm kind of looking forward to going."

"Well, I reckon it isn't that difficult to make perfumes," Dr. Trifle said. "I'll bet I could whip up a lovely fragrance in no time."

"I think you'll find that it's not that easy."

"We'll see about that," Dr. Trifle said, heading for his workroom.

"Perfumes," Selby thought. "I don't understand them. Why can't people just smell like people? Why do they waste so much money trying to smell like something else? I mean, I'm a dog and I smell like a dog. What's wrong with that?"

For the next few days the most revolting smells drifted out of Dr. Trifle's workroom. Finally, Dr. Trifle appeared, smiling, and holding three small bottles.

"Ta-da!" he sang. "The House of Trifle is proud to bring you Smell-O-Scents, a new concept in perfumes."

"A new concept?" Mrs. Trifle said, very suspiciously. "What *are* you talking about?"

"The thing about ordinary perfumes," Dr. Trifle said, "is that they usually just smell nice. They have the scent of roses, or jasmine, or camellias."

"What do yours smell like?"

"My Smell-O-Scents don't smell like any one thing. They *remind* you of places—tropical islands, mountain peaks, rivers. They don't just cover up people smells."

"I'm not sure I'd know the smell of a tropical island if I sniffed one," Mrs. Trifle said.

"That's because they don't have just one smell. They have lots of smells all together. Some of the smells are horrible and some are nice. When you mix them together in the right amounts something wonderful happens."

"Are you talking about scents? Or are you talking *non*-scents?" Mrs. Trifle laughed. "Get it? Scents? Nonsense?"

"Yes, very funny, dear," Dr. Trifle said, holding up one of his bottles. "But have a whiff of this."

Mrs. Trifle sniffed it and suddenly a smile spread across her lips.

51

"Mmmmmmm," she said. "That's very interesting. It reminds me of something."

"What?" Dr. Trifle asked eagerly.

"Rafting down a river."

"Smell-O-Stream," Dr. Trifle said. "That's what I've named it. You see, it works!"

By now Selby had made his way quietly up to Mrs. Trifle's side and had sneaked a secret sniff.

"Crikey!" he thought. "It's true! It reminds me of wild rivers and forests. Dr. Trifle is very clever."

"Here, try another one," Dr. Trifle said.

Mrs. Trifle dabbed a drop of the next perfume on her wrist and sniffed it.

"Deserts," she said. "Dry, wind-swept places. Red rocks with bits of blue grass growing between them. And lots of sand."

"She's right," Selby thought. "That's what it reminds me of too!"

"Smell-O-Sand," Dr. Trifle said. "And now try this one."

"Tropical islands come to mind," Mrs. Trifle said. "That's the best one."

"Smell-O-Surf," Dr. Trifle said proudly.

Selby put his nose close to the bottle and drew a deep breath and closed his eyes.

"I feel like I'm lying on a yacht," he thought, "anchored off palm-covered islands. People are bringing me plates of delicious food. Dr. Trifle isn't just clever—he's a genius! These Smell-O-Scents are fantastic!"

"Goodness, look at Selby," Mrs. Trifle said. "I think he likes that one. I guess we'll never know what it reminds him of."

"I'd better get back to work on Smell-O-Snow, my mountain perfume," Dr. Trifle said. "But I think I'll take a bottle of the Smell-O-Surf along to the launch tonight to show these House of Pierre people. Maybe they'll want to buy the formula from me."

That evening, the Trifles and Selby were met by Pierre de Paris himself as they entered the Bogusville Bijou Theater.

"Good evening," he said as hundreds of people filed past them. "I am told that you're the mayor of this lovely town."

"Yes, and this is my husband, Dr. Trifle," Mrs. Trifle said. "He has a little something to show you— his new perfume."

"A perfume-maker in Bogusville? This is impossible!"

"I'm just an amateur; a dabbler," Dr. Trifle said. "Or, should I say, a *dabber*, since we're talking about perfume."

"How very interesting," the man said stiffly. "But show me later. And please, no dogs."

"Selby will behave himself," Mrs. Trifle said.

"It is not the behavior but the odor," Pierre said, pinching his nose with his fingers. "Little doggies smell like . . . little doggies. He will cause confusion to the noses."

"Confusion to the noses? Doggy odor?" Selby thought. "What does this perfumed fancy pants want me to smell like: an ostrich?"

"Selby, I'm afraid you'll have to stay here," Mrs. Trifle said, giving Selby a pat. "Sorry."

"Oh, great," thought Selby as the Trifles went into the theatre. "Why couldn't they have just left me at home? I could have watched TV or read a book or something. I'll tell you what, I'm not sitting around out here."

When everyone was seated, the music began, the lights dimmed, and Selby crept into the hall.

"Nobody will notice me back here," he thought. "And I can watch the show just like anyone else."

For the next half hour one beautifully dressed model after another came to the middle of the stage, turned around twice, and then walked off again. Each time another model appeared, Pierre's assistants sprayed a different perfume in the air and Pierre said its name slowly and deeply into his microphone: "Suspense," he said. "Shadows . . . Melancholy . . . Excitement."

54

Finally it was time for the big moment. The hall went completely black, a drum played a drum roll and suddenly the air was filled with a different perfume. A murmur of excitement went through the audience and then the spotlight fell on Pierre, standing in the middle of the stage.

"And now, the moment we have all been waiting for!" he said. "The House of Pierre proudly brings you—Composure!"

"Composure?" Selby thought, sniffing a big sniff. "It smells more like compost. Smell-O Surf is so much better than any of these P.U. de Paris perfumes. It's all a big con."

When the clapping died down, Pierre cried, "Tonight, ladies and gentlemen, and tonight only, we have decided to slash our price and give you Composure at the special, once-only, low, low figure of only ninety-nine dollars and ninety-five cents!"

"One hundred smackeroos!" Selby thought. "That's outrageous! All that money for a tiny bottle of smelly liquid! What a rip-off! Forget the perfume; this Pierre guy is really beginning to get up my nose!"

But before these thoughts were out of Selby's brain a few people dashed up to the stage and began buying the perfume.

"It would almost be worth giving away my secret

just to be able to shout out, 'Don't buy that stuff; it's a waste of money!' Hey, now wait a minute! Hold the show! I know what I'll do."

Selby crept down under the seats till he was under Dr. Trifle's seat. Very slowly, and without the doctor noticing, Selby put his snout down in Dr. Trifle's jacket pocket and grabbed the bottle of Smell-O-Surf gently in his teeth. In a minute he had placed the bottle on a table at the back of the theater and had the cap off.

"Now all I have to do is move the table over in front of the air conditioner," Selby said, pushing the table, "and I'll give them a whiff of something really good."

Selby stepped outside the door again as the smell of tropical islands spread through the theater. Suddenly there were *ooooos* and *aaaaaahs* all around.

"What is that heavenly smell?" someone cried.

"It reminds me of ocean breezes and coral reefs," someone else said. "I feel like I've just gone on vacation."

"Forget the Composure stuff, Mr. Pierre," a woman said. "Where can we buy some of this?"

Dr. Trifle searched his pockets for the bottle. Soon one of Pierre's assistants located the bottle of Smell-O-Surf, sniffed it, and put the lid back on.

"Whose perfume is this?" Pierre demanded.

"I'm terribly sorry," Dr. Trifle said. "I'm afraid it's mine."

"Yours?" Pierre said. "Why did you want to ruin my beautiful launch?!"

"I—I didn't," Dr. Trifle said. "I don't know how it got there. Honestly, I don't."

Selby chuckled to himself as everyone crowded around Dr. Trifle.

"Where can we buy this beautiful fragrance?" they demanded.

"I don't have any more," Dr. Trifle said. "Only what's in that bottle. I guess I could make some more though. It's really not difficult to make."

"Get out of here, all of you ungrateful people!" Pierre screamed. "You are stupid, uncouth country people! You know nothing! I have wasted my time with you! Out! Out!"

Everyone filed out of the theater. Pierre was standing stiffly in the doorway as Dr. and Mrs. Trifle went out.

"We're terribly sorry," Mrs. Trifle said. "We really don't know what happened."

"I will tell you one thing," Pierre said. "I am never coming back to this terrible town!"

"I quite understand," Dr. Trifle said politely, adding, "Oh, by the way, may I have my perfume back?"

"I don't know where it is," Pierre said.

"But one of your assistants had it," Mrs. Trifle said.

"Then it is a mystery," Pierre said, blowing his nose in his silk handkerchief. "He must have thrown it away."

"Never mind," Dr. Trifle said, "I can make some more."

"That guy's lying," Selby thought. "One of these guys has Dr. Trifle's perfume. Now they'll take it back to their laboratory and figure out how to make it. He's just stolen Dr. Trifle's formula! And now Pierre will make zillions of dollars from it! Crumbs—and it's all my fault."

Just then, Selby smelled a faint smell of Smell-O-Surf. For a second he was back in the tropics lying on the beach. In his daydream he got up, stretched, and looked up at the coconuts in the palms above him.

"I'd love a nice sip of coconut milk," he thought. "Maybe I'll just climb up and pick a coconut."

In his mind, Selby leapt halfway up a palm, only to have it fall to the ground under his weight.

Selby came back to reality with a start.

"Get that savage dog off me!" a voice cried. "He's trying to kill me!"

Selby opened his eyes and there was Pierre lying on his back on the floor under him.

"Goodness, Selby," Mrs. Trifle said. "Get off that man. What's got into you?"

Mrs. Trifle was pulling Selby back by the collar when suddenly Dr. Trifle's perfume bottle rolled out of Pierre's pocket.

"Just as I suspected," Selby thought. "That scoundrel had it all the time!"

"I believe we've just located the bottle," Dr. Trifle said, picking it up. "Come along, Selby. I think you've solved our little mystery."

"So I have," Selby thought. "Come to think of it, maybe I'm not such a bad sniffer-dog, after all."

The Enchanted Dog

"Oh look," said Mrs. Trifle, who was reading the latest copy of the *Sisters of Limelight Every-Two-Weekly Newsletter,* "the Bogusville Stagestompers are doing a play called *The Enchanted Dog* and they need a dog for the title role. I think I'll take Selby to the audition to see if he can get the part."

Selby's ears shot up. "I've always wanted to act," he thought.

That afternoon Mrs. Trifle took Selby to the Bogusville Bijou where the author and director of the play, Melanie Mildew, who was also the gardener at the Bogusville Memorial Rose Garden when she wasn't writing and directing plays, was just starting the first rehearsal.

"Will he sit when you ask him to?" Melanie asked Mrs. Trifle.

"Yes, of course," Mrs. Trifle answered.

"And will he come when he's called?"

"Well, yes, I think so."

"He'll be perfect," Melanie said. "Just leave him with us."

"It doesn't sound like a very demanding part," Selby thought. "But it'll have to do."

"Attention everyone," Melanie said, clapping her hands above her head. "We have a dog. We can begin. Now let me tell you about the play. It's about a truck driver who comes to a sheep farm which is owned by three sisters who are really witches. They need a dog to drive their sheep. So they invite the trucker in for dinner, feed him some peanuts that they've cast a spell on, and then play some music that turns him into a sheepdog."

"Great stuff!" thought Selby, who was really getting into the swing of things.

"The big scene is when the trucker—that's you," Melanie said to Postie Paterson, the postman, "tries to break the spell by dancing *The Dance of Darkness.*"

"Why does he want to break the spell?" Selby wondered. "What's so bad about being a dog?"

"What you do is this," Melanie said. "You eat the peanuts and then stagger out of the house into the moonlight and fall behind that rock over there. Selby will be hiding there and all you have to do is push him out into the spotlight while you change into the dog suit. When you've got the suit on, you call Selby back behind the rock and then we cut the spotlight and you do *The Dance of Darkness*. The stage will be very dark and you will look just like a real dog dancing around. Okay? So *The Dance of Darkness* breaks the spell and the three sisters turn into ostriches and go running off. End of play. Everybody got it?"

"Let's see," Selby thought. "First I sit still behind the rock. Then I stand in the spotlight. Then I go back behind the rock and sit some more. Not a great part but I'll see what I can do with it."

"All right, then," Melanie said. "Places everyone. Let's give it a run-through."

On opening night a full house watched in silence as the Stagestompers performed the first act of *The Enchanted Dog* and Selby waited behind the rock for his big moment. The magic of the play began to bring out the actor in him, and he felt his heart throb when Postie Paterson gagged on the enchanted peanuts and staggered towards him.

Not waiting to be pushed, Selby leaped out from behind the rock as soon as Postie fell behind it. He jumped into the spotlight and stood there on his hind legs, turning from side to side so the audience could get a good look at him.

"This is wonderful!" Selby thought, and the excitement of the moment surged through him sending shivers of delight up his spine.

Then from behind the rock he heard Postie Paterson whisper: "Pssssssssssst! Here doggy. That's enough."

But instead of just walking back behind the rock as the spotlight went off, Selby leaped high in the air, jumping over the rock and hitting Postie squarely on the back as he bent down to put on the pants part of the dog suit. Postie went down with a crash, hitting his head on the floor.

"Postie!" Selby whispered, risking giving away his secret. "Are you okay?"

But there was no answer and in a moment a murmur rose from the audience as they wondered what would happen next.

"You are caught in our web of darkness," one of witches said for the third time. "You will never escape from us now."

The murmur soon grew to a mass of whispers and then Selby called out in a voice that sounded just like the postman's: "I will break your spell forever. I will dance *The Dance of Darkness* and be forever free."

Selby danced out in the half-light of the stage, whirling and twirling as the audience fell silent again. He leaped about as the music grew louder, feeling its beat flow through him. The audience gasped at the sight of the shadowy dog-figure and from the back of the stalls someone cried out, "Brilliant!" and another, "What acting! What dancing!"

Selby danced faster and faster; first on all fours, then on his hind legs and then leaping from leg to leg at blinding speed. Suddenly—just as the music stopped and the curtain began to fall—Selby saw Postie Paterson begin to come to. He leaped back behind the rock just as the house lights came on. The audience stood up and shouted "Bravo! Bravo!" and Melanie Mildew dashed across the stage and threw her arms around Postie Paterson who had just staggered out from behind the rock.

"You were fabulous!" she cried. "What a dancer! And that dog suit was perfect! You looked more like a dog than Selby!"

"Don't let it go to your head," Selby thought, feeling more proud of himself by the moment.

"But . . . but," sputtered Postie Paterson, holding his aching head with both hands, "I can't remember a thing. The only part of *The Dance of Darkness* I remember is the darkness part."

In the Spirit
of Things

"This house is haunted," Mrs. Trifle said one evening as she and Dr. Trifle sat watching a TV program called *Australian Spirits, Then and Now,* which was hosted by the famous ghost hunter, Myrene Spleen. "I keep hearing footsteps running in the hall at night and there's no one there. I'm sure it's a ghost."

"It's probably just Selby getting up to nibble a dog biscuit," Dr. Trifle said.

Selby's ears shot up like rockets.

"I'm not the one making the noises," he thought. "At night I tiptoe around like a cat so I won't wake the Trifles. But of course it can't be a ghost because there aren't any such things."

"It can't be Selby," Mrs. Trifle said. "He tiptoes around like a cat. No, I think it's a ghost and I'm going to ring Myrene right now and see what she can do about it."

Three days later Myrene Spleen raced down the Trifles' driveway carrying a large box that said *Ghost Hunter's Kit* on the top. "Spleen's the name and spooks are my game," she said, giving Mrs. Trifle a bone-crushing handshake. "Take me to the spirit spot and I'll get to the bottom of this, lickety-split."

"Whatever it is, it runs up and down the hall and makes a racket," Mrs. Trifle said.

"That's spook-like behavior all right," Myrene said, snatching a bucket from the box. "And I can feel its presence."

"You can feel a ghost?" Dr. Trifle said, looking at his hands.

"I get all tingly when there's a spook around," Myrene said with a shiver. "By the way, I did some research before I came to Bogusville, and it's my guess you're being haunted by none other than the ghost of Brumby Bill."

"Brumby Bill?" Dr. Trifle said. "But he built the first house in Bogusville. He's been dead for years," he added, suddenly realizing what he'd said.

"Precisely. He came to this area a hundred years ago with his dog to get away from the city. Gradually other people settled here and built houses," Myrene said. "You don't have to tell me about Brumby Bill, I know his story back to front."

"But why would he want to haunt us?" Mrs. Trifle asked, wondering why anyone would want to know a story back to front.

"My theory is that he hates what Bogusville has become."

"But Bogusville hasn't become anything," Mrs. Trifle said. "It's just another country town."

"It was unspoiled country when Brumby Bill lived here and now he thinks it's ruined. And who better to haunt than you, the mayor," Myrene said, pouring a tin of white paint in the bucket. "He thinks that he can scare *you* away and then the whole town will pack up and go. Would you like him exorcised?"

"Heavens no. He gets quite enough exercise dashing up and down the hall."

"Not *exercise, exorcise*. Exorcism is just a fancy word for getting rid of a spirit. How about it?"

"Well, yes, I suppose so," Mrs. Trifle said, wondering why ghost hunters didn't use simple words like everyone else.

"Won't you need television cameras and electronic ghost sensors and super-sensitive, quadro-gyric, scintillating, movement-activated microphones?" asked Dr. Trifle, who liked fancy words as much as anyone.

"The best way to catch a spook is to splash him with a bucket of paint," Myrene said. "It's an old-fashioned method but it usually works."

"Won't the paint go right through him?" Mrs. Trifle asked, wondering how she would ever clean the paint out of her carpets.

"Not if it catches him when he's not looking. I'll wait till I feel his presence with my psychic powers and then pull the rope that tips the bucket. *Glop, slop*—down comes the paint. Then I'll snap the photo. Ghosts don't like to be photographed. He won't be back after that. And don't worry about your carpets," Myrene added. "This paint washes off in water."

"I guess it's worth a try," Mrs. Trifle said. "Anything to get a good night's sleep."

"That's the spirit!" Myrene said, giggling after she said it. "Now lock that dog out so he won't get in the way. And you and Dr. Trifle can go to bed. I'll do the rest."

"Ghosts, schmosts," Selby said as he lay under a bush in the front garden. "Locked out of my own house just because of a silly ghost hunt. If I don't freeze out here, I'll starve. I'm so hungry I could even eat a Dry-Mouth Dog Biscuit!"

Selby climbed up the tree next to the side window and peered in at the ghost hunter who sat in the hall with her camera in one hand and the rope in the other.

"Psychic powers, piffle!" Selby thought. "The woman's sound asleep and she thinks she's going to catch a ghost. What rubbish! Whether or not she knows it," Selby added, "the Trifles left this window unlocked and Myrene's about to have a visitor."

Selby eased himself onto the window ledge and then slowly raised the window. He leaned in and put a leg in front of Myrene's face, waving his paw in front of her.

"A ghost could be doing a tapdance in front of her and she'd sleep through it," he thought. "That does it, I'm going in for a bite to eat, ghost hunt or no ghost hunt."

Selby crept down the hall to the kitchen and quietly crunched a couple of dog biscuits.

"If only I could just stay inside for the night," he thought. "Only then the Trifles would figure out that I opened an unlocked window and climbed in. They'd know they weren't dealing with an ordinary dog and it would be just a matter of time till my (gulp) secret would be out. Oh, well, out in the cold I go."

Selby was heading back down the hall when the sleeping Myrene Spleen suddenly jumped to her feet and yelled, "I've got the feeling! I've got the feeling! He's here!" And with this she pulled the rope.

"Help!" Selby screamed as the paint hit him with a *glop* and a *slop* and Myrene's camera flashed at the same time. "Get me out of here!"

He tore down the hall, hurled himself through the air—narrowly missing the screaming woman—and dived out the open window.

"I'm finished!" he said, hosing off the paint with the garden sprinkler. "It's over. As soon as they look at that photo they'll know that I climbed a tree and broke in through the hall window. I'm done. I'd better go and confess right now."

Selby slunk towards the front door just as Myrene burst out on the way to her car.

"Look at the dog!" she screamed, waving a photograph at Dr. and Mrs. Trifle. "I was wrong. It wasn't the ghost of Brumby Bill. It was the ghost of Brumby Bill's dog!"

Selby stared at the picture of himself, covered in paint, leaping through the air toward the window.

"It's the first dog ghost that's ever been photographed! And a talking dog ghost, too! Did you hear him say, 'Get me out of here!?' He won't be back to haunt you. This is great! It'll be my best TV show yet!"

"That was a close call," Selby thought as he lay on the hall carpet a little later with his eyes closed, ready for sleep. "I can't wait to see Myrene Spleen on TV talking about the dog ghost and holding up that picture of me covered in paint. Well, at least I can sleep in the house again *(yawn)* now that this ghost nonsense is over."

Selby listened as the footsteps walked along the hall, passing so close to his head that he felt a slight breeze from the moving legs.

"That'll be Dr. Trifle *(yawn)* heading for the kitchen to get a drink of water," he thought. "He often does that in the middle of the night."

Had Selby lifted his head at that moment and opened his eyes to look down the darkened hall, searching for the shape of Dr. Trifle hurrying along in his dressing-gown; had he just lifted one eyelid a crack, as he did when he didn't want anyone to know he was peeking, instead of falling into a deep sleep, he'd have seen *that there was no one there.*

The Screaming Mimis

"Bushfire love, yeah yeah, bushfire love," Selby sang along with the latest video clip by the rock super-group, The Screaming Mimis, as he danced around in front of the TV. "That Mimi, the lead singer, is great! And, what's more, the group is coming to Bogusville tonight! I've got to find a way to get into the Town Hall to see them!"

That night Selby ran down to the Bogusville Town Hall just in time to see The Screaming Mimis unloading the equipment from their van. He looked around for a way into the hall but there were guards at every entrance holding back screaming fans.

"If only I could get past the guards and then hide under a table till the show starts," Selby thought as he watched the band come and go through a back door. "How will I do it?"

For a moment, everyone was in the hall and Selby jumped in the back of the van.

"Hmmmmmmmm. What's this?" he said, pulling at the sides of a big wooden box. "They must have equipment stored in it. If I can only get in it . . ."

The box was nailed shut but some of the nails had come loose and Selby pried the side open and hopped in, hitting a mass of wires.

"Phew!" he said, pulling the side closed again after him. "There's barely enough room in here for me." He was peering out through the tiny holes in the sides of the box when Mimi and her drummer, Slam-Bam Benson, got in the back of the van.

"Help me carry the box, Slam-Bam," Mimi said in a tiny, high-pitched voice.

"Cripes!" Selby thought. "That's Mimi. But what's happened to her voice? She doesn't sound anything like her records."

Mimi and Slam-Bam lifted the box out of the van and began carrying it inside.

Suddenly Mimi put her end of the box down.

"I can't take it any more!" she blurted out. "Driving all day, working all night—we've been on the road for six months and it's just too much! I can't sing tonight. I can't!"

"Please, Mimi. We can't go on without you," Slam-Bam pleaded. "It's the last night of the tour. We can't cancel on our last night."

"I don't care. I'm squeaking like a mouse," Mimi said, wiping away a tear. "If I don't sing 'Bushfire Love' at the top of my voice, the audience will feel cheated. And I can't do it."

"Don't worry," Slam-Bam said. "We'll turn the amps way up."

"It won't be enough," Mimi said. "Listen to me. I can hardly talk."

"Speak up, I can hardly hear you," Slam-Bam said.

"I *am* speaking up," Mimi said in a voice not much louder than a whisper.

"Don't worry, Mimi," Slam-Bam reassured her. "We live in the age of electronic wizardry. We'll turn the amps way up and that'll do till we get to 'Bushfire Love.' Then we'll connect up the Super Computerized High-Pitched Ear-Piercing Brain-Scrambling Sound Blaster. It'll make a whisper sound like a stick of dynamite."

"I don't know . . ." Mimi started.

"Trust me, Mimi. I built it myself and I tell you it can do everything except sit up and sing," Slam-Bam said, "and I'm working on that."

"Wow!" Selby thought. "A Super Computerized High-Pitched Ear-Piercing Brain-Scrambling Sound Blaster! I can't wait to hear it."

"No offense, Slam-Bam, but I don't trust it. We

77

haven't used it before in a concert," Mimi said as she peered down into the holes in the box, not quite seeing the dog-figure lurking in the darkness inside. "Besides, it's been bouncing around in the van so long, it's falling apart. Look, the nails are coming out."

"That's nothing. I can fix that in a second," Slam-Bam said.

And before Selby could say, "Oh no, I've just climbed into a Super Computerized High-Pitched

Ear-Piercing Brain-Scrambling Sound Blaster without realizing it," Slam-Bam dropped his end of the blaster and gave the loose nails a whack or two with his hammer—which would have been okay if Selby's head hadn't been right up against the side of the box. He got such a good banging that he didn't remember a thing till three paragraphs from now.

"There, it's fixed," Slam-Bam said. "It'll really blast the rafters, you wait and see."

"I warn you, Slam-Bam," Mimi peeped. "If it doesn't work tonight, I'll put an ax through it."

Selby awoke that evening to the deafening sound of drums and screaming teenagers. He peered out through the holes and saw the flicker of lasers in the air.

"Now for our final song," Mimi squeaked as she connected up the sound blaster. " 'Bushfire Love!' "

"Oh, no!" Selby thought as he peered out of the blaster and then scratched and pushed with all his might. "If I don't get out of here fast, this Super Computerized High-Pitched Ear-Piercing Brain-Scrambling Sound Blaster's going to pierce my eardrums and scramble my brains for sure!"

Slam-Bam hit a drum and Selby bounced off the inside of the blaster, his fur standing on end, then collapsed in a heap, his ears ringing like church-bells.

79

"I've got to do something fast!" Selby thought. "If he hits that drum again, I'm gone! My secret doesn't matter any more. It's a matter of life and death! Help!" Selby screamed in plain English at the top of his lungs. "There's a talking dog stuck in the sound blaster—and it's me! Let me out!"

But Selby's screams were nothing but a peep as the drummer sent another and another beat through the blaster.

"I've got to destroy this contraption before it destroys me!" Selby thought as he grabbed a mouthful of wires and pulled them, covering himself in a shower of sparks.

"That's done it!" he thought. "I've disconnected the blaster. Now all I have to do is wait till someone opens it."

Mimi sang soundlessly for a second and then gave the blaster a whopping great thump with her boot.

"I told you it wouldn't work!" she cried. "It's a useless piece of junk."

With this she grabbed a fire ax and raised it over her head, ready to chop the blaster in two.

"Gulp," Selby said, staring up at the ax. "This is not the way I wanted the blaster to be opened. I've got to do something before that crazy crooner gives me the chop!"

And with this he screamed out the chorus to

'Bushfire Love' as loud as he could, imitating Mimi's voice:

> Ain't cryin' out for you no mo'
> My love is burnin' on a ten-mile front
> Clearin' a firebreak with my eyes
> You are the backburn of my heart.
> Bushfire love, yeah yeah
> Bushfire love . . .

Mimi stared at the blaster as Selby sang on and on, louder and louder.

"I can't believe it," she said, scratching her head. "That box is singing my song!"

Selby finished the song to a roar of applause. And before he realized what he was doing, he took a deep bow, sending the blaster tumbling off the stage and onto the darkness of the dance floor below, where it broke open.

"I can't believe it either," Slam-Bam said. "I said that contraption could do everything but sit up and sing. I was wrong—it sat up and sang."

"And in quite a good voice," Selby said as he ran across the crowded dance floor and out the exit. "Even if I do say so myself."

Selby in Love

It was a sunny spring day and Selby lay in the shade of his favorite bush, finishing a book he'd found called *Love Dawns Eternal*. A warm wind sprang up just as he read the last paragraph.

> *For a year I'd worked for Howard Cooper, the master of Cooper's Rest. He was a man both silent and strong. Howard, whose dark looks cried out for a woman's love, my love. And now, as I was about to board the coach and leave forever, I turned back a loose strand of hair and Howard caught a glimpse of my rose-colored fingernails. Then his eyes penetrated my soul and he gently clasped my hands. His quiet voice whispered in my ear, "Oh Dawn, my rosy-fingered Dawn, you are the one I've waited for these many years. Please don't go. Stay on and be my wife."*

"Oh, that sends shivers up my spine," Selby said with a sigh. "Imagine. For all that time Howard didn't even notice her and then his eyes penetrated her soul *(sigh)* and he fell instantly in love *(sigh)*. Oh, isn't love wonderful," Selby thought as he tripped lightly into the house and lay dreamily on the carpet. "I only wish it could happen to me. Why can't I find someone like Dawn to fall in love with?"

And then it was that Selby heard out of the corner of his ear, Mrs. Trifle say to Dr. Trifle, "Did you know that your old friend, Ralpho, is having a rather successful tour of country towns?"

"Ralpho? *The* Ralpho?" Dr. Trifle asked, referring to his old friend Ralpho the Magnificent, failed inventor and sometimes magician. "I thought after so many disastrous shows, he would have gone out of the magic business for good."

"For everyone's good," thought Selby.

"He not only didn't quit," Mrs. Trifle said, "he seems to have added a talking dog to his act."

"A talking dog?" Selby wondered. "How can it be? I'm the only talking dog in Australia and perhaps the world."

"A talking dog?" Dr. Trifle asked. "How could it be? There aren't any talking dogs in the whole world—not even in Australia."

"There's an article about Ralpho here in the newspaper," Mrs. Trifle said, holding up a copy of the *Bogusville Banner.* "In it he says Lulu was found—"

"Lulu?"

"His talking dog. The article says that Lulu is a real, live talking dog who was found walking aimlessly in the jungles of the Amazon."

"That's the sort of thing Ralpho might say to get people to go along and see his act, don't you think?"

"Well, maybe," Mrs. Trifle said. "But if that's true, he's managed to fool everyone in the towns he's been to on his tour and Melanie Mildew as well."

"Melanie Mildew?" Dr. Trifle asked.

"She's the one who wrote the article," Mrs. Trifle said, "and I don't think she's easy to fool."

"Gulp," Selby thought, "neither do I. I wonder if there could be any truth in this."

"I just wonder if there could be any truth in this," Dr. Trifle said. "I guess we'll have to trot along tonight and see for ourselves."

"Yes," Mrs. Trifle said, "and Ralpho asked us to bring Selby along. Why not, he might enjoy it."

That night the Trifles and Selby sat in the front row of the Bogusville Bijou as Ralpho's show went terribly wrong. First one of his juggling rings got caught on a light and wouldn't come down. Then he tried to juggle three bowling pins but one hit him on the head and the other two landed on his toes. And when he talked to his ventriloquist's dummy his mouth was moving so much that the audience screamed with laughter, making it impossible for anyone to hear anything.

"Quiet please!" Ralpho yelled as he put the dummy away and got out a whip. "Now if I may have a volunteer from the audience I will demonstrate how I can take a pencil out of someone's mouth at ten feet with the crack of this whip. Come on, speak up. Who will it be?"

For a minute, no one moved and then a voice cried out, "Well it won't be me! Fair crack of the whip, Ralpho, you'd take my head off and leave the pencil!"

"Poor Ralpho," Selby thought as the audience burst into laughter, "he's just not a showman."

"Okay," Ralpho said, pulling out a pistol, "I guess that brings us to the trick-shooting part of my act."

Suddenly there was a stampede for the exits which only stopped when Mrs. Trifle leaped to the stage and grabbed the microphone.

"Come back, everyone! Please! Order! Order," she yelled. "Ralpho's not going to do his trick-shooting act, are you Ralpho?"

"I don't know why no one likes my trick shooting," Ralpho muttered to Mrs. Trifle. "It's always so exciting. I think so anyway. Okay, I'll bring out the talking dog and finish the act."

"Ladies and gentlemen," Mrs. Trifle said, stepping aside, "can we have a big hand for Lulu the talking dog!"

Ralpho reached down and lifted a small dog onto the table in front of him.

"Hmmmmmm," Selby thought, pricking up his ears. "That doesn't look like a stuffed toy. It looks like the real thing. But of course it can't be. It'll be interesting to see how Ralpho fakes the talking part."

Ralpho pulled a watch out of his pocket.

"Excuse me, folks," he said, looking at his watch, "but I've got a train to catch in just a few minutes and I don't want to miss it.

"Now let me tell you about Lulu. She was found wandering aimlessly in the jungles of the Amazon by a butterfly collector from Ballarat who later sold her to me," Ralpho said. "He was on his way out of the jungle after collecting seventy-two new species of butterfly when he happened across her. He reached down to pat her and she said in perfect English, 'Excuse me, sir, but I'm lost.' Didn't you, Lulu?"

"That's correct," the dog said suddenly in perfect English.

"It's got to be a trick. She's hardly moving her mouth," Selby thought, suddenly remembering that he hardly moved his mouth when he talked. "She can't be a real talking dog. There simply aren't any—well, except for yours truly."

"Tell the audience more about yourself," Ralpho said.

"There isn't really anything to tell, Mr. Magnificent," Lulu said. "I have amnesia and can't remember anything before I met the butterfly collector."

"So there you have it, folks," Ralpho said. "The only talking dog in the world!"

"My goodness," Dr. Trifle whispered to Mrs. Trifle loud enough for Selby to hear as well. "This is the most sophisticated piece of gadgetry I've had the pleasure of seeing. I wonder how he's doing it? I think we can rule out the use of a super high-frequency oscillating converter."

"Can we?" Mrs. Trifle asked.

"Yes. And we can also rule out lambda wave transmission through thixotropic media."

"Are you sure?"

"Absolutely. And he couldn't be using smart-quark excitation because I don't suppose he's ever even heard of it," Dr. Trifle said.

"Do you know those silly dolls that have a string you pull to make them talk?" Mrs. Trifle asked. "I think it's one of those."

"Hmmm, good point," Dr. Trifle said, looking for a string but not seeing any.

"I know what you're all thinking," Ralpho said, glancing at his watch again. "You think that Lulu has a string I pull to make her talk. Not true, is it Lulu?"

"No, it certainly isn't, Mr. Magnificent," Lulu giggled.

"And now, ladies and gentlemen," Ralpho said, "I need a different sort of volunteer. Could you please bring your dog up here, Dr. and Mrs. Trifle?"

Mrs. Trifle picked up Selby and put him on the table next to Lulu.

"Hello, how are you?" Lulu said, and Selby felt himself go all weak at the knees.

"I can't believe it," Selby thought as he looked deep into Lulu's eyes. "It sounded like she actually spoke to me!"

Ralpho looked at his watch for a moment and then said, "What do you think of the mayor's dog, Lulu?"

"He's very handsome," Lulu said, batting her eyelids.

"I can't believe it!" Selby thought. "Here I am face to face with another talking dog! A friend at last! Maybe even a girlfriend!"

"I think he thinks you're very pretty," Ralpho said.

"Do you think so, Mr. Magnificent?"

"Oh, wonder of wonders!" Selby thought. "This is the most beautiful day of my life."

"Go ahead, little doggy," Ralpho said to Selby. "Don't be shy. Talk to her. She won't bite. Ha ha ha."

The audience giggled and then burst into spontaneous applause.

"Lulu is a thinking, feeling, and talking dog just like me!" Selby thought. "I've got to talk to her before Ralpho races off to catch that train. But—but—but if I do my secret will be out. Who knows— I could end up in Ralpho's show!"

"I like you," Lulu said, blinking her eyelashes at Selby. "Do you like me?"

Selby saw a tiny smile cross Lulu's lips and his mind raced like a speeding train.

"Oh, no! Her eyes just penetrated my soul!" he thought. "If I don't talk to her now I'll miss my chance. She'll never know that there's another talking dog in the world!"

Selby was just about to say: "My name's Selby and I believe that you and I are the only talking dogs in Australia and perhaps the world," when suddenly Lulu said, "Thank you for sharing your thoughts with me, with me, with me, with me—"

90

There was a murmur in the crowd as Ralpho kicked something under the table and then there was a terrible scratching noise.

"It's not a talking dog at all!" someone screamed. "Ralpho's got a record-player under the table! Look!"

"I see!" Dr. Trifle said to Mrs. Trifle. "He knows exactly when she's going to speak and he asks her questions just before she answers. It's the oldest trick in the book."

"Thank you, ladies and gentlemen," Ralpho said, turning bright red and running off with Lulu as the audience roared with laughter.

"It's a pity about that record-player getting stuck," Mrs. Trifle said later when they were walking home. "Poor old Ralpho almost had me believing that there was a real talking dog right here in Bogusville."

"Yes," Dr. Trifle said. "He certainly gave us all something to think about for a minute or so."

"One more minute," Selby thought as he trotted ahead, "and I'd have given them something to really think about!"

Selby Unstuck

"Look! Come quickly!" Mrs. Trifle cried.

Dr. Trifle came dashing into the study with Selby right behind him.

"What is it, dear?" the doctor asked.

"A great discovery!" Mrs. Trifle said, holding up an old postcard. "I found this in the middle of that book about Canada. I suspect that your great, great, great-grandfather, Fred Trifle, wrote it to your great, great, great-grandmother, Matilda, before they were married."

Dr. Trifle held up the postcard and read it:

September 15, 1857

Dear Matilda,
*   The weather is here, wish you were beautiful. Ha, ha. Great joke, isn't it? See you soon.*
*   Love, Fred*

Dr. Trifle looked puzzled as he re-read the card.

"Yes, very interesting," he said, finally, "but that's the oldest, corniest postcard joke in the world. Instead of writing, 'The weather is beautiful, wish you were here,' he wrote 'The weather is here, wish you were beautiful.' Get it?"

"Of course I get it," Mrs. Trifle sighed. "You used to write it on every postcard you sent me before we were married, remember?"

"Did I?"

"You did."

"Come to think of it, I did," the doctor chuckled.

"Well, it wasn't funny then and it isn't funny now."

"But you used to tell me how funny it was."

"I was being polite," Mrs. Trifle said. "But it isn't the message on this postcard I wanted you to see; it's the stamp."

Dr. Trifle looked at the stamp.

"Hmmm," he hmmmed. "It's a triangle with a picture of flying ducks on it and it says 'Newfoundland' and 'Two Pence' on the bottom. It's a strange one, all right. It could be worth a fortune."

"A *double* fortune," Mrs. Trifle said. "The ducks were printed upside down by mistake. An old stamp with a mistake on it must be very, very rare and very, very valuable. Let's take it to a stamp expert and see how much it's worth."

"Speaking of corny old jokes," Dr. Trifle said. "Our comedian friend Gary Gaggs is a bit of a stamp-nut and we're going to his comedy show tomorrow night, remember? Maybe he can come back here afterward and tell us what the stamp is worth."

"Good idea."

That night, when the Trifles were safely in bed, Selby crept into the study and had a good look at the stamp.

"What a great find!" he thought. "I wonder if the Trifles are going to sell it? I'd sell it in a second! Wow, all that money! Goody, goody! What a great vacation they could have!"

The next day everyone in Bogusville had heard about the rare stamp. Soon there were newspaper people and TV crews knocking at the door to interview the Trifles and to take pictures of the postcard. "I don't like everyone knowing that there's something so valuable in the house," Dr. Trifle said that evening. "Someone might break in and steal it. And we can't insure it because we still don't know how much it's worth. Maybe we should have kept it secret for a few days."

"Don't worry, dear. I'll put it in our bank vault

tomorrow. In the meantime, I'm sure it'll be fine right here in this book."

That evening the Trifles went to Gary Gaggs' comedy show and Selby stayed at home.

"This rare stamp business was so exciting at first," Selby thought, "but now it gives me the shivers. I hope nothing happens while the Trifles are away."

No sooner did these words trickle through Selby's brain than there was the crash and tinkle of breaking glass in the other room.

"What was that?" Selby wondered. "Could it be someone breaking in?"

It could and it was: into the study climbed two men wearing black burglar masks. Selby ducked out of sight around the corner before they noticed him.

"Is this the place?" one of the burglars asked the other.

"Yeah, this is it all right," the other said.

"Okay, let's get to work and find that stamp."

Selby heard the burglars pulling books from the shelves.

"I found the postcard!" one of the men said, finally. "We're rich! Come on, let's get out of here!"

"Oh, no!" Selby thought. "The Trifles are about to lose the stamp! I can't let this happen!"

Suddenly Selby remembered an article he'd seen

about burglaries and burglar alarms.

"Some of the best burglar alarms are the ones that have recorded voices," he remembered. "They yell things out and the burglars think that someone's at home and so they go running off."

Just as the burglars turned to go back out the window, Selby yelled out the first thing that popped into his head: "All right, you two! This is the police! Come out of that room with your hands up!"

"The cops!" one of the burglars whispered.

"It can't be!" the other one whispered.

"It is. They must be in the living room."

"Okay, don't shoot! We give up!" the first one called out.

Slowly the burglars came into the living room with their hands in the air. One of them was holding the postcard.

"Oops! I did it wrong," Selby thought. "I should have just told them to drop the postcard and get out! What do I do now?"

The burglars looked around the room and then one of them put his hands down and started laughing. He went over to Selby and patted him on the head.

"What's so funny?" the other one asked.

"You, you dummy. Can't you see there's no one here but this dog?"

"So where are the cops?"

"There aren't any cops. It's just one of those stupid burglar alarms. Someone put the wrong message on it. They should have said, 'Get out before I call the police,' or something like that. What a ninny!"

Suddenly Selby remembered something else from the burglar article.

"The best burglar alarm is a dog," he remembered. "Hey, That's me! I'm a dog! I'm a burglar alarm! I should be barking and snarling and biting and all those other dog-like things! But wait, if I do that now, they'll run off with the stamp! Why didn't I do it before they found the stamp?"

But Selby noticed that the burglar with the postcard was holding it right next to his nose as he patted him. Slowly and secretly Selby's tongue slid out and touched a corner of the stamp. In a moment he'd wet it through and had a loose corner of the stamp in his teeth. He pulled gently, and then he pulled not so gently, and finally he gave it a yank and a jerk and the stamp slipped into his mouth and was safely hidden under his tongue.

"Hey! The dog's got the stamp!" the burglar yelled. "Grab him!"

Selby turned and let out a flurry of barking and growling so ferocious that he even frightened himself.

"Hey! This dog's going to kill us!" the other burglar yelled. "Let's get out of here!"

The two men ran back into the study and dived through the window as Selby ripped at their clothes.

"That was good fun!" Selby squealed when the burglars were safely out of sight. "Now all I have to do is glue the stamp back on the postcard and put the books back on the shelves. The Trifles will know that someone broke their window but at least they'll have their stamp."

Selby opened his mouth to spit the stamp out but nothing came out. He moved his tongue around and around searching for it and then went to the mirror, opened his mouth, and gazed in.

"It's gone!" he cried. "While I was barking and growling, I swallowed the stamp! By now it's completely dissolved. Oh woe, woe, woe!"

That evening the Trifles arrived home with Gary Gaggs who made straight for Selby and began patting him.

"I love your dog," he said. "I used to have a dog myself once. It was a black dog—but then again, it wasn't a black dog."

"How is that possible?" Mrs. Trifle said.

"It's simple: he was a *grey*hound," Gary said, pumping his arms up and down, strutting around like a rooster and saying, "Woo woo woo!" as he always did when he made a joke.

"That's very good," Dr. Trifle said. "You never stop, do you?"

"But seriously, folks," Gary went on, "his name was Dale. I tried to take him up in a plane with me but he wouldn't go. You see he wasn't an *Aire*dale. Woo woo woo! But speaking of stamps, you do know the difference between a woman and a stamp, don't you?"

"Well, I think so," Mrs. Trifle said, wondering why there was a draft coming from the study.

"One of them's a *female,*" Gary said, "and the other one's a *mail fee.* Woo woo woo!"

Just then, the Trifles noticed the broken window

and the stampless postcard lying on the floor.

"Someone's stolen the stamp," Mrs. Trifle cried. "We were so silly! Why didn't we just take it with us?"

"Calm down," Gary Gaggs said. "From the way you described it, the stamp was just a Newfoundland Two-penny Triangle. I'm afraid they aren't worth anything. They printed tons of them."

"But this one had the ducks printed upside down," Dr. Trifle explained.

"Worthless," Gary said. "They were *all* printed with the ducks upside down. Well—almost all. The stamps with the ducks rightside up are the valuable ones—there are only three of them left in the whole world."

"Well, thank goodness for that," Dr. Trifle sighed. "I guess some burglar is in for a big disappointment."

Gary turned over the postcard, read the message and then burst out laughing.

"Get a look at this!" he said. "'The weather is here, wish you were beautiful.' That's great!"

Mrs. Trifle frowned.

"Haven't you heard it before?" she asked. "It's the oldest postcard joke in the world."

"Of course I've heard it," Gary said. "The point is that this was written in 1857. It's probably the first time that joke was ever used. Your great,

great, great-grandfather probably made it up! I'm going to recommend that the International Jokes Library in Gulargambone buy this postcard for their collection."

"What an interesting idea," Dr. Trifle said. "Do you suppose they'll pay us a fortune?"

"I doubt it," Gary Gaggs said. "But they'll probably pay you enough to buy a decent burglar alarm."

"A burglar alarm," Mrs. Trifle said. "What a good idea."

"Burglar alarm, schmurglar alarm," Selby thought as he licked some threads out of his teeth. "What you need is what you've already got: a good old barking, biting, and *thinking* dog—me!'

AFTER WOOD or
THE EPIC LOG

Dr. Trifle finally got that huge log into his fireplace and now he and Mrs. Trifle are sleeping soundly on the couch. So now I can write another note.

I hope you liked these stories about me. Most of them are true, but you know how writers are—they always make stories a bit better than they already are. So don't believe every word you read. Anyway, I forgive the author for not telling the truth all the time and I hope you will too.

One thing I told him to lie about is Bogusville. It's a real town in Australia but Bogusville isn't its real name. I made it up so no one would find me. I also lied about Dr. and Mrs. Trifle's names. That would be a dead giveaway if they ever saw this book. Oh, and one more thing. My name's not Selby. That would be a giveaway too. My name could be Spence and I could live with the MacWilliams of Mudgee. Or I could be Patches and live with the Catalanos of Benalla. (I'm not telling.) Of course I could be your dog. So go ahead and say "I know it's you, Selby. I know you understand every word I say." But please forgive me if I don't answer.

Life is great just the way it is and I'm not going to spoil it.

 Selby